THE CASE OF THE STRAY STICKPIN

THE KITTY WORTHINGTON COZY CAPERS, BOOK 2

MAGDA ALEXANDER

CHAPTER 1

SEPTEMBER 1923, LONDON

LADIES OF DISTINCTION DETECTIVE AGENCY

"Bam, bam, bam, bam." Someone not content to ring the bell to our detective agency had decided to pound repeatedly on the door.

How very annoying! Somewhat in a tiff, I slung open the door to find Lord Marlowe on our doorstep, nattily dressed in a bespoke 3-piece navy blue suit, his chestnut mane in wild disarray from the blustery day. In other words, magnificent as always.

The observation, however, was not reciprocated. "What the blazes have you done to your hair?"

"I've cut it." I fluffed my do to show off my bob. "Do you like it?"

His brow knitted. "It's ... different."

Coming from him, it was the closest to a compliment I

would ever receive. "That it most certainly is. Would you like to come in?" I held the door open wide.

"I would." Without further ado, he stepped in and hung his fedora on the hat stand.

Two months earlier, Kitty Worthington and I had started the Ladies of Distinction Detective Agency, counting on word of mouth to gain us business. But that had not turned out to be the most propitious of times. Most of high society had fled town in August, eager to return to their country estates to hunt, ride, and have a jolly good time at house parties.

So as things stood, we had to depend on clients who either spotted our sign over the door or noticed our adverts in the newspapers. Unfortunately, those were few and far in between. As a consequence, we were bleeding red ink and spending much more than we were taking in. If this kept up, we'd have to close up shop before the season started again in March. I, for one, dreaded that outcome for it would mean a return to my dreary existence in Hertfordshire with the rest of my family. I would do anything to avoid that fate, including welcoming the maddening Lord Marlowe to our agency.

"Would you care for a tour?" I tossed him a smile.

His mouth scrunched. "If that's what you wish."

What had put him in such a foul mood? "We don't have to if you'd rather not."

"No, please, lead on. I would love to explore your new agency." He'd improved his attitude a tad, probably to be polite.

"Splendid."

The townhouse, located off Hanover Square in a mixed residential and commercial neighborhood, was classy without being ostentatious. Our reception area consisted of one sofa, a settee, two very comfortable chairs, and a smattering of small tables. Kitty's mother had donated them as they'd been tucked away in her attic collecting dust. The family's contributions did not stop there. The Duke of Wynchcombe, Kitty's future brother-in-law and a noted botanist, had provided potted plants from his conservatory which brightened up the space no end. The result was both charming and cheery.

"The ground floor consists of a reception area plus our two offices, one each for Kitty and me. A small kitchenette for tea and such, and, of course, a WC."

"How suitable." He glanced around. "Where is Miss Worthington?"

"She's discussing a possible case with a client." Kitty was visiting a Mrs. Grimes whose poodle had been dognapped from Belgrave Park. Earlier this morning, the dog owner had telephoned in tears about her missing Gigi. Too distraught to leave the house, she'd asked Kitty to come to her Belgravia home. Once Kitty heard the word Belgravia, she knew Mrs. Grimes was well off. So she'd packed her stylish satchel with her usual investigative tools and set off in her brand new roadster to visit the grieving lady.

"How is the agency faring?" Lord Marlowe asked.

"As well as can be expected. We are a new business after all." I wasn't about to reveal our state of financial distress when he'd strongly disapproved of the agency to begin with. He believed ladies should marry and pop out babies on a regular basis, not work as a sleuth. Or any other profession for that matter.

"That's good to hear." He turned back in my direction, and a whiff of his citrus cologne drifted over to me.

Goodness! The man could make me weak in the knees. But no matter how delicious he smelled, I needed to keep my professional demeanor. Putting some distance between us, I led the way up to the next level. "This floor contains a conference room, another WC, and a small library." The books had come with the house as the son of the previous owner, who'd died rather unexpectedly, had not wished to cart them off. While most of the tomes were downright stodgy, some were of an unusual nature which made us wonder about the activities of the previous occupant. But since Kitty's brother Ned had arranged very favorable terms for a one-year lease, we did not object to the books remaining. At the very least, they would occupy space in the shelves. As long as no one glanced at the titles too closely, they made us appear well read.

He glanced up. "What about the top floor?"

I folded my hands in front of me. "Those are my private rooms."

His gaze snapped back to me. "You're living here? By yourself?"

"Who else would I be living with, Lord Marlowe?"

He pursed his lips, disapproval evident in that shapely mouth of his. "A single lady living by herself without a chaperone? That's just not done."

I sniffed. "It is now." I purposefully glanced at my watch. "I'm afraid that's all the time I have right now as I'm extremely busy." I wasn't, as there was little to do. "May I show you the way out?"

His pointed gaze drilled into me. "This is not a social call. I want to hire you."

"To do what?" I snapped out, rather churlishly I'm afraid.

"I've misplaced my tie clip. It's a family heirloom and very valuable. I want you to find it."

My heart skipped a beat. A client! And one who would pay well. Changing my attitude, I offered him my brightest smile. "Well, in that case, let's proceed to my office." We descended the wooden stairs, my heels clacking while his steps echoed a sounder tread. Once we arrived in my office, I

THE CASE OF THE STRAY STICKPIN

retrieved a blank journal from my desk. Whenever the agency took on a new matter, we employed a new one to record all the details of that case.

"Name?" Of course, I was thoroughly familiar with it, but I wanted him to say it out loud.

He arched a brow. "You know my name, Emma." He'd dropped the Lady to which I was entitled to since I was the daughter of an earl. But rather than comment about his breach of etiquette, I decided to ignore it. He was about to become a paying client, after all.

"Nicholas Devlin Wollscroft, Earl Marlowe. Address, 14 Grosvenor Square, Mayfair, London." I glanced at him. "Now, if you will, please describe the tie clip."

"I just did," he said, stretching out his crossed legs and flashing his superior grin.

Patronizing to say the least, but I paid no heed to it. "In full detail, please. The more information we have, the easier it will be to locate it."

"It's a rectangular base with a wolf's head. Gold, of course. Emerald eyes. It was a gift to my father from his father."

I'd seen it on him before. A rather hideous thing if you asked me, but there was no accounting for taste. "About two inches in length, isn't it?"

"Just about."

His fingers drummed on the arm chair, which got on my nerves no end. But I kept my composure. "When was the last time you saw it?"

"Yesterday, at my gentleman's club. I was wearing it when I entered but noticed it was missing when I climbed into my Vauxhall Tourer." The motorcar he was inordinately fond of.

"How far was your vehicle from the club?"

"Fifteen feet or so. I was parked by the kerb directly in front. Before you ask, I retraced my steps. It was nowhere to be seen."

"Did you inquire at your club about it?"

"Of course I did," he huffed. "What kind of an idiot do you take me for?"

When I remained silent while staring at him, he continued, "They haven't found it."

"What time did you arrive?"

"About noon. I was set to have lunch with Lord Meecham."

"What is the name of your gentleman's club?"

He appeared insulted by the question. "Black's, of course." The premier gentleman's club, patronized exclusively by the creme de la creme of British high society. No common folk need apply.

"Very well." I blotted the ink. "I believe that's all the details I require at the moment. We will inquire about it and contact you within three days with a progress report."

"Very well."

"Now as to the matter of our fee, we require a retainer of twenty pounds."

The drumming fingers came to a halt. "Twenty pounds? That's rather rich."

He was not being a skinflint, only careful. After inheriting an estate which had been almost bankrupted by generations of spendthrift ancestors, he'd managed to parlay his annual income into a quite respectable fortune. Most of it was managed by Worthington & Son, the financial investment firm that Kitty's father owned.

But no matter his objection, business was business. I was right to demand a retainer from him. "Our daily fee is a pound a day. There are also bound to be additional expenses. All incurred in your service, of course."

His gaze narrowed. "What sort of expenses?"

"Well, since only gentlemen are allowed in Black's, we

will have to employ a male associate who can breach those hallowed halls."

"Who?"

I hadn't the foggiest, but Kitty probably would. She had connections with certain elements of society who were eager to perform tasks, whether they were legal or not. For a fee, of course. But Lord Marlowe didn't have to know any of that. "I'm afraid that's confidential information, milord. I'm sure you appreciate the need to protect our sources."

"Yes, well." He had no ready answer for that, as there would be none.

"I'll need the twenty pounds in cash."

"I usually don't carry money on my person. I will send my private secretary tomorrow."

"Very well, milord." I slammed shut the journal. "We will start our inquiry as soon as we receive the retainer."

His air of superiority vanished. "You should start immediately. You know I'm good for it."

I hitched up my chin as I was not about to give in an inch. "This is the way we do business, milord. If you don't appreciate how we operate, you're more than welcome to seek the services of another detective agency." Too late I regretted my unruly tongue. We were in desperate need of income, after all.

He leaned forward. "That won't do, Lady Emma. I want you," he spit out through gritted teeth.

He was in a snit. And all because I'd demanded a retainer in cash. Assuming a businesslike tone, I said, "We will await your private secretary then."

"You shall have it within the hour." With that he came to his feet, grabbed his fedora, and stormed out, almost barreling into Kitty at the front door.

"Lord Marlowe!" she said, surprise evident on her face.

"Miss Worthington. My apologies." He briefly nodded before rushing off.

Kitty stepped into my office, a question mark written all over her face. "What on earth?"

"I know. Isn't he the drollest?" I was laughing so hard tears were running down my face.

She tossed a glance toward the front door. "What has gotten into him?"

I had no desire to explain the battle of wills I'd just endured, so I simply said, "Haven't the foggiest. But he made for an entertaining afternoon, I'll give him that. More importantly, he retained us as a client."

Her gaze bounced back to me. "Did he really? What for?"

"He wants us to find a tie clip he lost at Black's. You've seen it. The one with the wolf's head."

Her nose wrinkled "That ugly thing? Why would he want it back?"

"A family heirloom, or so he says. I asked him for a twenty pound retainer."

She barked out a laugh. "You didn't! We usually only ask for five."

"Well, I know he doesn't carry cash on him. So I wanted to see what he would do."

"You are—"

"Ingenious?"

"Most definitely." She removed her gloves and tossed them into her handbag.

"How did your interview with Mrs. Grimes go?"

Over the next few minutes, she gave me a summary of her discussion with the lady. Once she'd done so, we proceeded to the Tea and Tattle to celebrate our new enquiries.

CHAPTER 2

A PRIVATE CONSULTATION

The first order of business was to recruit someone with knowledge of the hallowed halls of Black's. Of course, not just anyone would do.

One name came to mind, Dickie Collins, a gentleman Kitty first met on the Golden Arrow. After he'd provided a service which helped her solve a case, she'd asked her father to find a position for him. He was now employed at one of the best restaurants in the City of London. As he belonged to a league of servers employed at the finer establishments, he was likely to know someone who worked at Black's.

The following morning, I sent a note to his address. That afternoon, he telephoned with the name of a contact. The server in question would be happy to discuss our enquiry. For a fee, of course.

I wasted no time contacting the gentleman, and we agreed on a time and place to meet. As he was required to work from noon until late in the evening, he suggested eleven the following morning at a public house close to his residence. As it was situated a fair distance from Black's, he wouldn't encounter anyone he knew.

I arrived fifteen minutes early to case out the place and was happily impressed by what I saw. Not only was the enterprise clean, but so were the customers and staff. At the appointed hour, Mister Aloysius Clark made an appearance. Having never met before, I'd devised a way to recognize each other. I was to tuck a red rose in my hair, while he wore one on his lapel. Rather clandestine, but it did the trick. As soon as he spotted me, he made his way to my table.

Mister Clark had to have some Nordic blood in him for he was tall, broad, and his hair bordered on white. When the waitress approached to take our order, I treated him to Shepherd's pie. He chose a ginger beer as Black's frowned on the staff smelling of alcohol.

"Thank you for seeing me," I said.

"You're welcome." He cleared his throat. "As I told Dickie, I won't do anything illegal."

"Not to worry, Mister Clark. We require all associates to adhere to the law." Anyone we hired to assist with an investigation had to sign an agreement to that effect. A protection of sorts. If they subsequently decided to circumvent the law, we could prove we'd specifically required them not to do so.

"That's good," he said.

"Have you learned anything?" After he agreed to talk to me, I'd asked him to do a spot of investigation. So hopefully he had something for me.

"Lord Marlowe lost it two days ago, just as he said. The Black's staff has searched high and low for it, milady. I don't believe it's there."

"He said he had it on when he arrived. Could it have fallen off in the cloakroom?"

"Not according to the attendant. He searched for it that day and again yesterday."

"Lord Marlowe enjoyed a luncheon that day with Lord Meecham. I understand you were the server."

"Yes. They enjoyed a beef Wellington with roasted potatoes and a bottle of burgundy. The meal was put on Lord Marlowe's account."

"Did you overhear their conversation?"

"We must keep their conversations private, milady," he said somewhat chagrined.

"Yes, I know. I promise not to tell anyone, not even Lord Marlowe." I had to find out what had been discussed. I had a hunch it was important. "I'll add a bonus if you tell me." I would list the expense as 'information received' on Lord Marlowe's invoice without revealing the source.

He glanced around the pub, probably to determine if there was anyone familiar to him. He must have been satisfied with what he saw because he soon answered, "They were discussing a financial matter. Lord Marlowe had lent Lord Meecham some funds, and he hadn't paid it back. Lord Meecham asked for more time."

"How did it end?"

"Lord Marlowe gave him a thirty-day extension to repay the money."

"You think they would have had this discussion in a more private setting."

"Apparently, Lord Marlowe had tried to arrange for such a meeting, but Lord Meecham had been hard to pin down."

"Did you hear any details about the loan?"

"The money was to be used to pay off some debts related to Lord Meecham's estate." The look on Mister Clark's face appeared to doubt that explanation.

"But you don't believe him?"

"Well, he's been losing money at the tables."

"Cards?"

"Yes, milady. He visits the card room at Black's at least twice a week and engages in games of whist. He's not very good at it. Loses money regularly."

"And probably returns again and again to try and recoup his losses."

"Exactly, milady."

"Does Lord Marlowe ever play cards?"

"Occasionally. But he wins most of the time. He has a very sharp mind."

It was good to know Marlowe was not an inveterate gambler.

"If I may, milady, about Lord Meecham."

"Yes."

"Lord Marlowe is not the only gentleman Lord Meecham owes money to. There are others. Just last week another gentleman was pressing him to pay off his debt. He was leaving for the continent and wanted the debt settled."

"So not only can't he repay Marlowe, but others as well."

"Yes, milady."

"Lord Meecham is in dire straits indeed."

"I don't suppose I can ask you to spy for me."

"No, Milady. I could lose my job."

"Yes, of course."

"There is one more thing," Mister Clark said.

"Yes?"

"Lord Marlowe's pin is not the only item that's gone missing."

CHAPTER 3

THE INVESTIGATION ADVANCES

"So several items have gone missing from Black's?" Kitty asked. After my luncheon with Mister Black, I'd returned to the agency. Finding her there, I shared what I'd discovered with her.

"According to Mister Clark," I replied.

"We haven't heard about such a thing happening. The papers certainly haven't reported it."

"Well, most of the gentlemen attending Black's these days are city men—financiers, successful businessmen and such. They wouldn't want to advertise their losses. I imagine they're conducting their own investigations."

"Could the staff be stealing from the members?" Kitty asked.

"Or one of the members himself," I said.

"Lord Meecham?"

"I don't see how at least as far as Lord Marlowe is

concerned. It's a stickpin. How do you reach into a gentleman's lapel and steal it."

"Maybe he removed his jacket."

"Gentlemen don't do that in a gentleman's club." Or so I'd been told.

"Do you know if he did?"

"No, I don't. I'll have to ask Marlowe. I'll send him a note."

"A personal consultation would be better," Kitty suggested.

Suspicion rose in my mind. "Why are you so eager for me to see him in person when a note would do?"

She harrumphed. "Written missives don't provide the opportunity to gain greater knowledge. Lord Marlowe might come up with another idea or share something else. A conversation is best."

"Ummm." She was right. I needed to discuss the matter with him. I could only hope he would be in a more amiable mood than he'd been two days before.

Following her advice, I telephoned Lord Marlowe to request an audience. He suggested we meet at his address at noon the next day. We could enjoy a spot of luncheon before our meeting. His suggestion was not outrageous. After all, if I were a gentleman, instead of a lady, I would be expected to attend him at his home, not have him drop into our detective agency. Inappropriate as it was for a lady to enjoy a private luncheon with a gentleman at his residence, I agreed with his suggestion.

Upon my arrival at his home, I was shown into his study. The furnishings were classical Georgian furniture—dark, heavy, but magnificently constructed. He was dressed in yet another three piece dark blue suit with a pinstripe waistcoat, a dark blue tie, and a matching pocket square. The epitome of a well-dressed gentleman.

"Lady Emma." He bowed. "Thank you for agreeing to

meet me here. Won't you take a seat?" He pointed to a round table and the dark blue chair comfortably situated next to it. "I requested a light luncheon be served. Chicken a la Parisienne, accompanied by Potatoes Lyonnaise, and a raspberry trifle for dessert. I hope it meets with your approval."

Most of the time, I ate a sandwich for lunch, so this was sumptuous fare indeed. "It sounds delicious."

"I can assure you, it will be. My chef trained at LeCordon Bleu." No sooner had he said that than the study door opened, and several servants strolled in. Rather than presenting dishes from which we could help ourselves, they delivered the meals already plated. After a white wine was approved by Lord Marlowe, they departed. The entire procession had taken but a few minutes.

"I prefer our luncheon to be private as there may be confidential things we will be discussing."

"Most assuredly." The chicken with its rich sauce smelled heavenly and tasted even better. By mutual agreement, we did not discuss the purpose of our meeting but kept the conversation light, much of it dealing with the agency and our mutual acquaintances. But once the dessert was served and the coffee had been poured, I deemed it time to begin our discussion. I detailed what I'd discovered so far.

"Not much progress," he said after taking a sip of his brew.

"It's early days. What did you discuss with Lord Meecham during your meeting with him?"

"Why do you ask?"

"It may have something to do with the case, of course." When he hesitated, I said, "I will keep what you say confidential. No one will ever know."

He raised a doubting brow, but he answered, nonetheless. "I lent him a thousand pounds. He said he needed it to settle estate debts. He was to pay it back two weeks ago. When he didn't, I requested he settle his loan. That's when I discovered the funds did not go to that purpose. He had lost money playing cards. I took him for an honorable man. More fool me."

"You didn't know about his card playing?"

"I knew he dabbled but didn't know the extent of his losses. I trusted his word the funds would be used for his estate. He has a younger sister and a widowed mother. He's awfully young himself, barely twenty three. I gave him the benefit of the doubt. In hindsight, I realize I shouldn't have."

"So what happens if he doesn't pay you back?"

He shrugged. "Chalk it up to a bad debt. I can withstand the loss."

Who knew Marlowe had such a tender heart? "About the pin. You wore it on your lapel."

"Yes."

"Did you remove your jacket while you were in the club?"

"Of course not. A gentleman does not do that kind of thing."

"And you definitely had the pin on you when you entered the club?"

"Of course I did. I put it on that morning."

"And you went directly from here to the club?"

He scrunched his brow. "Yes. I said so, didn't I?"

"Could it have had a loose clasp?"

"No."

"Your valet didn't notice such a thing?"

"He was a bit under the weather. I dressed myself that day."

"You could have fastened it wrong."

"I've done it hundreds of times, Lady Emma. I would have known if there was something wrong with the clasp."

"Very well. So we've ascertained you were wearing it

THE CASE OF THE STRAY STICKPIN

when you arrived at your club. But it was missing when you left."

"Yes."

"What did you when you entered the club?"

"I was greeted by the doorman. I proceeded to the cloakroom to check my hat and my coat. I stuffed my gloves into the coat pocket."

"The pin was still on you."

"As far as I know. I did not particularly notice."

"And then what did you do?"

"I proceeded to the dining room. Lord Meecham was already seated at our table. He came to his feet as soon as he saw me. We shook hands. The server took our order, served water. I ordered a burgundy to accompany the beef Wellington. I enquired about Lord Meecham's family, his mother and sister. But waited until our meal was served to inquire about repaying the loan. Our conversation regarding that topic did not last long. He said he couldn't repay for the moment and asked for more time. I gave him a thirty-day extension. Once the meal ended, I came to my feet. I had an appointment outside the club. We shook hands once more, and I left. I then retrieved my coat, hat and gloves and walked to my automobile. It was rather brisk outside. So I decided to slip into my outer coat. That's when I noticed the stickpin was missing from the lapel. Is that thorough enough for you?"

"Quite. The thing is, Lord Marlowe, that you can't account for the stickpin being on your lapel before you entered the club. It could have fallen out anywhere in your home or in your car."

"I thought of that. My staff has performed a thorough search. It's not here. Neither is it in my automobile."

"It could have fallen during the walk to your automobile."

"I don't see how. I was wearing my coat when I left this

house. Even if it had become loose, it would have been caught by the coat."

"And you went directly from here to the club?"

"Yes."

"You did not stop for petrol, or your bank, or visit a particular friend?"

He quirked a brow at me. "No. The chère amie was the after-luncheon appointment."

I narrowed my gaze at him.

"I don't have a chère amie, Lady Emma. I had an appointment with my banker at two. I can have him call you to confirm it if you wish."

"No, that won't be necessary." I sighed. "Well, it does seem as if the stickpin disappeared within Black's." The problem was how to prove that. Mister Clark refused to do anything which would jeopardize his position. I didn't blame him. Other servers would more than likely have the same mindset which meant I could not get help from someone inside the club. I would need to devise another scheme.

CHAPTER 4

A SCHEME IS PROPOSED

"You could always disguise yourself as a gentleman and infiltrate the club," Kitty suggested once I explained my dilemma.

Trust her to make an outrageous suggestion. "Are you insane? I could never pass myself off as a man." With no clients present, we'd accommodated ourselves in the reception area of the Ladies of Distinction Detective Agency to discuss our respective cases.

"Why not? All it will take are new clothes, a deeper voice, shorter hair."

"I'm not cutting my hair!" I loved my profession as a Lady Detective, but I refused to alter my looks for the sake of an investigation. Besides, I'd already had it shaped into a bob.

"You won't have to. You can wear a wig." She studied me while slowly strolling around me. "Your walk needs to change as well. No swinging of hips."

The statement offended me. Unlike some females who

exacerbated their gait to attract the male gaze, I took pride in doing no such thing. "I don't swing my hips."

She laughed. "Yes, you do, dear Lady Emma. It's your natural stride. All women have it. Men walk straighter, taller. Stand up." Once I did, she said," Now walk from here to the reception area and back again as a man."

I did my best to do just that.

"That won't do," Mister Clapham said. A former Scotland Yard detective inspector, now employed by us, he provided not only the experience and knowledge we lacked but the male perspective. He'd joined us while we discussed our cases.

I whirled toward him. "Why not?"

"Because you're still walking like a woman."

I breathed out a frustrated breath. "Fine. Tell me how to do it."

"Walk to your office. Shoulders back, stiffened spine. No swaying. One foot in front of the other."

I started to do just that.

"No swaying," Kitty reminded me.

"I'm not," I protested.

She put her hands on my hips from behind. "Now walk."

When I did, she scrunched that part of my anatomy. "Point your feet forward, not to the side. Straighten your spine. Now do it again."

I practiced again and again and again until both were satisfied. By the end, my feet were sore, my back hurt, and my shoulders throbbed. "How do men do this?"

"It's their natural walk," Kitty said. "Women have hips for childbearing which of course necessitates the, ahem, hip swings."

"Will you stop talking about it? Now what about clothes?"

"You'll need a dark suit," Mister Clapham said. "I know just the place. It caters to the server trade. What's your size?"

Once I told him, he took himself off.

"Here." Kitty tossed me my handbag. "We're going shopping."

The shop she chose catered to the gentlemen wig trade. Although initially surprised to find ladies in his store, the proprietor became totally accommodating once we explained our purchase would be for an uncle who was sick but wanted to welcome visitors with a full head of hair. Using my cranium as a model, I chose a dark haired wig that could be arranged into a conservative style.

After completing our purchase, we made our way out. "Should we return to the agency?" I asked.

"Not yet," Kitty said. "We have one more stop to make."

"Where?"

"There." She pointed to a storefront emblazoned with the words *The Silhouette Shop*.

Confused, I said, "I don't need undergarments."

"Yes, you do." She pointed to my upper torso. "Your chest. It will have to be flattened."

I gazed down. "I'm not generously endowed, Kitty."

She grinned. "You jiggle when you walk, dear Lady Emma. Or rather your breasts do."

As there was nothing I could say to that, I remained silent.

"Thank heavens that's the fashion these days," Kitty said. "It should take but a tick to find something suitable."

By the end of the day, I had a dark suit, gentleman's shoes, a dark wig, and a bust flattener.

In the changing room in the back of the agency, I changed into my disguise. One look in the mirror told me I'd achieved my goal. Pleased with the way I looked, I emerged triumphant and twirled, "Will I do?"

Kitty frowned. "What do you think, Mister Clapham?"

"The trousers need to be shortened. They're too long.

That wig doesn't do you any favors. And your anatomy"—he brushed a hand across his chest— "isn't quite right."

"The bust flattener needs to be tightened," Kitty said. "Here, I'll help you."

Back we went into the changing room where I stripped to my undergarments. Taking matters in hand, literally, Kitty pulled and fiddled with the torture device until my front was flat as a pancake.

"I can't breathe," I protested.

"Breathing is highly overrated. Now about your hair. What about a pompadour?"

As I could hardly draw breath, I wheezed out, "Fine."

Of course, she was not happy just to arrange the wig, she had to add one more touch—a pencil mustache. Where she'd gotten it was anybody's guess.

"It looks fake," I managed to say.

"Nonsense. You look dashing. Now go out there and show Mister Clapham."

He took a long time scrutinizing me, but in the end, he said, "You'll do. Except for your trousers. They're still too long."

"I'll alter them, Lady Emma," Betsy said. Formerly Kitty's lady's maid, but now our receptionist, she was a whiz with a needle.

"We seem to have forgotten one thing," I said, propping my hands on my non-swinging hips. "How can I work as a server at Black's?"

"Ask your contact to recommend you."

"What if he says no?"

"Offer him a financial incentive, Lady Emma. I'm betting he won't deny your request."

When I met with Mister Clark, we'd agreed I'd send him a note to the club if I required another meeting. After doing so, I settled down to wait. Two hours later, I had my response.

He would meet me at The Wounded Duck, a pub situated close to Black's, after his shift ended at eleven. Arriving early, I put in an order for a dark ale to pass the time until his arrival. He was thankfully on time.

"Good evening," I said. "Thank you for meeting with me."

"You're welcome."

"I have a favor to ask of you, one that would necessitate your recommendation."

He didn't say yes. But neither did he say no. "If you could please explain," he said.

"If I arrange for someone to reconnoiter for me, can you get him inside the club?"

"As a server, you mean?" he asked.

"Yes."

While he considered my suggestion, I tossed out the financial lure Kitty suggested. "You'd be appropriately compensated for your assistance, of course."

"How much?"

"Twenty pounds?"

His brow scrunched while he thought it over. "That's acceptable. A couple of the servers are ill, so the serving staff is shorthanded. I can recommend your associate to the club's assistant manager. He makes all the hiring decisions. Will you send a note with the details?"

"There's no associate, Mister Clark. The server you will recommend is me."

His eyes widened. He swallowed hard. "Milady. You couldn't possible pass yourself off as a gentleman."

"On the contrary, I already have. A previous investigation, you understand." A total fabrication, but he had to believe I could do it.

"I don't know." He was wavering. Afraid of losing him, I sweetened the pot.

"I'll pay you thirty pounds." That was more than he made in a year.

He gulped. It took but a moment for him to say, "I'll do it." The money had been too much temptation for him. "When would you like to start?"

"Tomorrow?"

He nodded. "I'll talk to the assistant manager first thing in the morning. What name shall I give him?"

"Thomas, Thomas Carr." The name of our family's stable master at our home in Hertfordshire. As a child, I'd often sought refuge at the stable from a loud family who talked incessantly without saying anything worthwhile.

"Arrive at eleven. And don't be late, mind you. The assistant manager is a stickler for punctuality."

"Will do. Thank you, Mister Clark. I appreciate what you're doing."

"You're welcome. I just hope I don't come to regret this."

"You won't." Easy to say, difficult to predict.

CHAPTER 5

BLACK'S, A GENTLEMAN'S CLUB

In the end, the interview lasted but a few minutes. A crisis had occurred in the club's main lounge, so all the assistant manager did was glance me over and nod. "Report to Mister Clark. He'll tell you what to do. Oh, and the job is only temporary, mind you. Once we're fully staffed again, we won't need your services."

"Yes, Sir. Thank you, Sir."

"Go on then."

He hadn't pointed out which way to go. But the aroma of delicious food imbued the space. Following the scent, I soon found the dining room. When I reached its entrance, Mister Clark rushed over. "How did it go?"

"I'm hired. Temporarily. He told me to report to you. The whole interview took but a few minutes. He said there was an emergency?"

"One of our older members had a turn, keeled right over.

The club doctor brought him around. But they're taking him to hospital."

"Oh, dear. I hope he recuperates."

"Yes. Well, let me show you around." He pointed to the room. "We've already set the tables—silverware, china, water and wine glasses, napkins—so you won't have to do that. Our maitre'd is ill, so I've been put temporarily in charge of the dining room."

"Excellent." With him as the head waiter, I'd be less likely to be found out.

"When a member enters, I will get the details. Is someone joining him? Does he prefer to sit at a particular spot? That kind of thing. I will then escort him to his table. To start with, you will observe me take his order and deliver it to the kitchen. While we're doing that, the busboy will bring a basket of rolls to the table and fill his water glass. The sommelier, Mister Hodgson, will then ask for his wine preference. After that, you'll be on your own. Now let me introduce you to the rest of the staff." That took but a few minutes, and then I watched while he waited on the next member to arrive at the dining room.

My first assignment came in the shape of a stout gentleman. "Please show Lord Stoughton to his table," Mister Clark said. "He prefers one away from the kitchen."

"Yes, Sir." Back stiffened, shoulders back, clutching my order book to my nonexistent bosom, I led the aristocrat to a spot on the far side of the room. Once he was seated, I said, "Good day, milord. My name is Thomas. I will be your server."

All I got in response was a grunt.

"Today the chef recommends the roasted croute spread with its own cooked liver, bread sauce, and red currant jelly, accompanied with game chips." Or so I'd learned in the kitchen.

THE CASE OF THE STRAY STICKPIN

The aristocrat blinked at me. "I'll have a steak, my good man. Blood rare, mind you. What a good Englishman eats. And fried potatoes, sliced, with lots of butter. Bring plenty of rolls too."

"Of course, milord."

He squinted up at me. "You're new here, aren't you?"

"Started just this week."

Another grunt.

"The sommelier will be here soon to take your wine order."

He dismissed my comment with a wave of his hand. "Tell him to bring me a bottle of the Cabernet Sauvignon 94. He knows the one I mean. He holds them in reserve for me."

"Of course, your lordship." On the way to the kitchen, I alerted Mister Hodgson, the sommelier, to the aristocrat's need.

"Bloody steak, fried sliced potatoes, with lots of butter?"

"Yes, Mister Hodgson."

"No manners that one. Feed him rare steak and fried potatoes, and he's as happy as a pig in muck. One day he'll keel over from apoplexy. Mark my words."

"Yes, Mister Hodgson."

His gaze raked over me. "Don't turn your back on him. He loves to pinch bottoms, especially sweet, tender ones like yours."

Well, that took me aback. "I beg your pardon?"

"Oh, you don't fool me, dearie. Trying to pull a fast one for a lark? Wouldn't be the first time."

My stomach sank. Fifteen minutes into the job, and I'd been caught. All I could think of saying was, "Please don't tell."

"No one to tell. Our maitre'd is out with some disgusting illness. Coughing up a lung, he was." Another pointed glance. "How long do you intend to do this?"

"A day or two."

"No more than that. Someone is bound to notice."

"Great Scott!" A loud voice reached us from the entrance of the dining room. One I recognized.

"I think someone just did. If you'll excuse me." The coward fled to the kitchen leaving me to face a very irate Lord Marlowe.

Mister Clark was attending to another club member, so I had no choice but to approach the earl. "Would you like a table, milord?"

"What the blazes are you doing here dressed like that?"

"Please lower your voice," I whispered before speaking in a much higher tone. "Right this way, your lordship."

"I don't want a bloody table," he hissed. "I want you to explain yourself."

Ignoring his words, I said, "A spot by the window. Absolutely. Please follow me. We have the perfect seating for you." Thankfully it was half past eleven so the dining room was only occupied by Lord Stoughton and a couple of other gentlemen. Once we reached the secluded spot, I said, "Here we are, milord. Would you like to see the menu for today." I handed it to him.

"It's indecent what you're wearing. I can see the shape of your bottom."

"Somehow I doubt you've never seen a lady's bottom," I hissed.

"Never in public, dressed like that."

"Then you must have gone blind, Lord Marlowe. Female trousers are becoming all the rage."

"What are you doing here?"

"What you hired me to do," I whispered through clenched teeth. In a much louder voice, I exclaimed, "I can recommend the braised pheasant with whisky sauce and pearl barley pilaf."

"I don't want—"

"Excellent choice, your lordship. The braised pheasant it is." And with that, I left him fuming. Honestly, how would I find out what was going on at the gentlemen's club unless I disguised myself as a man?

Rather than deal with more snipes from him, I asked the busboy to deliver his basket of rolls and butter while I proceeded to the kitchen to submit his order. And then as more members strolled into the dining room, Mister Clark directed me to a table of gentlemen, none of whom was less than seventy years of age. I treated them as kindly as I could while serving their food and drink. Thankfully, they were easily satisfied.

Lord Marlowe kept shooting me pointed glances and head nods. So much so, he appeared to have a nervous tick. Finally, when his order was ready, I brought it to him.

"Meet me in the library at two," he said. "We can talk there."

CHAPTER 6

A LIBRARY TÊTE-À-TÊTE

"How did you even get this position?" He asked.

"My informant recommended me. Two of the servers are ill as well as the maî·tre d so they're short on staff. I must say, it's been rather easy. No one suspects a thing." Except for the sommelier, that is. But Marlowe did not need to know that.

"That's because half of them are too blind to see. Your walk is a dead giveaway. No man swings his hips the way you do. And your scent? Did you drown yourself in cologne?"

Bristling at his remark, I hitched up my chin. "It's a manly scent. Citrusy, like yours."

"Not like mine. You smell like a woman to me."

"For heaven's sake, Marlowe! Would you like to hear what I plan to do? Or do you want to continue harping at me?"

His brow knitted while he glared at me. But then he answered, "Your plan."

"Your stick pin must have fallen off during the transfer of

your coat at the cloakroom, either when you were handing it to the attendant or when you retrieved it. I will be discussing this with him."

"When?"

"This afternoon."

"And you think the attendant is going to open up and share things with you, a stranger?" His tone dripped with sarcasm.

Honestly, he was impossible. "Yes, I do. My informant is having a word with him right now. I authorized him to offer the attendant a financial incentive."

"A bribe."

"A consultation fee. It will be properly accounted for in the invoice I send you."

"Of course, it will."

"I'll telephone you in the morning to share what he said."

We'd been standing by the bookshelves while we carried our conversation, but suddenly he took to wandering about the library. I would have loved to leave so I could check with Mister Clark, but I knew Marlowe well enough to know he was not through questioning me.

Sure enough, he soon turned back to me. "Out of curiosity, what do you do when you need to visit the loo?"

"I attend the staff one. There are buckets there for our use. So, I drop my trousers and do what must be done."

The expression on his face was priceless. I'd left him speechless.

"For heaven's sake, Marlowe, there are private stalls."

"And urinals where a male staff member will have his family jewels on display."

"As I have no desire to see a gentleman's privates, I don't look. Now do you want me to find your stickpin or continue this inane discussion?"

"Find it, of course."

"Wise decision. In addition to talking with the cloakroom attendant, I plan to remain tonight after hours so I can search the premises, especially the areas assigned to the staff."

"How do you know a staff member did not walk out with my stickpin the day it went missing?"

"Every one of them was searched that day. And so were their personal lockers. Ever since, the club manager has adopted the same modus operandi. Nobody leaves without their persons and belongings being searched. None of them could have gotten your tiepin out of the premises that day or any other day since."

"And you think you will find it in one of their lockers tonight?"

"I do not. But I must look. Once I'm done with those, I will search the rest of the building."

"How will you do that?"

"The club closes at midnight. I'll have five hours before the charwomen arrive to clean."

"Are you planning to hide somewhere in the building?"

"No. My informant will leave a window unlocked right here in the library. If you'll notice this room is in the back of the club and faces the mews. So, it's the least likely to raise suspicion when somebody enters through one of the windows. I should be able to slip in and out without anyone the wiser."

He crossed his arms across his chest. "There are two floors to the club. You'll need help."

"Well, unfortunately, Mister Clapham is otherwise occupied with Kitty's enquiry. So I'm it."

"I will assist you."

"No, thank you." He was bound to be more hindrance than help.

"I will meet you outside the library window at midnight."

THE CASE OF THE STRAY STICKPIN

"Marlowe," I said all gnashed teeth.

"Be reasonable, Lady Emma." His tone grew softer. He could be quite charming when he chose. "You can't do it alone."

He had a point. "Very well."

After leaving the library, I checked with Mister Clark. As we'd agreed, he'd arranged for me to talk to the cloakroom attendant at three. It being nearly that time, I headed in that direction. Unfortunately, the attendant had nothing of note to report. He had neither seen Marlowe's stickpin, nor noticed anyone taking it. He knew he was the most likely suspect. But he swore he hadn't taken it. He would never jeopardize his position by stealing the pin. He had a wife and a child to feed. After paying him the compensation I'd agreed on with Mister Clark, I returned to the dining room. Per my request, he'd drawn up a list of those present, both club members and staff, the day Marlowe's heirloom had been lost. I would need to discuss that list with Marlowe. While I felt comfortable questioning those who worked at the club, it would be difficult to do the same of the club members. We would need to discuss the best approach.

The rest of the day passed without my gender being discovered, my biggest fear. When my shift ended at eleven, along with the other servers I made my way to the assistant manager's office where I turned out my pockets and was patted down by him. As I was wearing my bosom constrictor, he didn't detect anything out of the ordinary.

It was downright pouring outside, so I snuggled into my gentleman's coat, popped open my umbrella, and headed to The Wounded Duck. I had to trust Mister Clark would leave the library window unlocked. At a quarter to midnight, I made my way to the mews and the back of the club building where I found Marlowe waiting for me.

He was wearing a coat, but no hat. As a result, his hair lay plastered to his head, his teeth were chattering, and he was shivering. He strongly resembled a drowned rat.

"Where the blazes have you been?" He barked out.

"In the warm confines of The Wounded Duck like a normal human being."

"Why didn't you tell me? I could have met you there."

"We can't afford to alert suspicion, Marlowe. A toff like you would stand out by a mile. What happened to your hat?"

"The blasted wind took it. Can we get in before I freeze?"

"Give me a leg up so I can reach the window."

"And what would you have done if I weren't here?"

I pointed to a stack of boxes resting against the building. "Drag one of those over. Go on."

Threading his hands, he boosted me up. Thankfully, Mister Clark had done his part. The library window was unlocked. After I climbed in, Marlowe grabbed the windowsill and raised himself up. I was impressed. His upper body strength was downright admirable.

"Let's search the lockers first," I said.

He nodded as he blew on his hands in an attempt to warm himself up. I waited until he stopped shivering before retrieving my torch from my inside pocket. To my surprise, he'd brought one as well. We were very thorough in our search. But as I expected, we did not find anything in the staff lockers or areas they frequented.

"What now?" He asked.

"We'll need to search the rest of the building. Start at the top and work our way down."

We did not discover anything even remotely suspicious on the top floor. When we moved our search to the lower floor, I suggested we start with the billiards room.

"Why?" Marlowe asked. Of course he did.

"Along with the library, it's one of the rooms that's not in plain view. Everyone can easily see others in the dining room and lounges. But in the billiards room, there are only two tables. And from what Mister Clark said, only one is in use most of the time. It would be easy for someone to stash something there without being seen."

We searched the tables and shook the billiard balls with no success. But when I stumbled into the rack of billiard cues, knocking several to the floor, one of them rattled.

"What was that?" Marlowe asked.

"A cue."

One at a time, we picked them up and shook them. I got lucky with the fourth one. "I think there's something inside."

"Give it here," he said. After I handed it to him, he fiddled with it and discovered it could be unscrewed. He tipped the part that rattled onto the billiard table. Out tumbled several pieces of jewelry, including his stickpin, an emerald ring, a Rolex watch, and a roll of cash. "By Jove."

"You found it!"

His triumphant gaze found me. "We found it."

"Let's check the rest." For the next several minutes, we did just that, but none of the others rattled, nor was Marlowe able to unscrew those cues.

"Well, that's that," he said. "Do you know if anything else has gone missing?"

"No. From what my informant said, only jewelry and cash. We seem to have found them."

"How many individuals suffered losses?"

"Four, including you and Lord Nesmith. He was playing cards with several gentlemen. One of them lost rather heavily. But Lord Nesmith is not one to accept vouchers. He insists on being paid in legal tender. The gentleman who lost settled up with him and left. From what I hear, Lord Nesmith simply stuffed the cash in his pockets. At the end of the evening, the cash had disappeared."

"How much money are we talking about?"

"Five hundred pounds."

"Not an insignificant amount." He counted the bills in his hand. "It seems to be all here, minus a pound or two. Did Nesmith report the theft to the police?"

"No. Mister Stafford, the club manager, reimbursed him for his loss in return for Lord Nesmith keeping mum about it."

"What about the other two items—the ring and the watch?"

"Mister Stafford asked those members for a fortnight's delay in reporting the missing items."

"And they agreed?"

"Well, they were assured a thorough investigation would be conducted. Neither wished to besmirch the reputation of the club."

"When did all this happen? Do you know?"

"The same day your stickpin went missing."

CHAPTER 7

PLANS ARE MADE

Marlowe decided to approach Mister Stafford the next day. He planned to inform him that he'd taken matters into his own hands and conducted a late-night search. And that he'd found his stickpin, other jewelry, and cash in a billiards cue.

As I was not scheduled to arrive until noon and he planned to request an audience shortly after the club opened at eleven, I did not hear about that discussion until he appeared in the dining room and requested me as his server.

"We need to talk," he said as soon as I showed him to a table, strategically located away from other members.

"Not right now. We're too busy." It being Friday, many of the City of London banker and business types had decided to enjoy their luncheon at Black's. So the dining room was full. As we were short on staff, I was being run off my feet taking orders and serving food. So I had no time to enter into a discussion with Marlowe.

"When will you be free?"

"Thirty past two." The lunch rush would have died down by then.

"Meet me in the library then."

We were allowed a fifteen minute break in the early afternoon, so I claimed it at that time. I walked into the library to find Marlowe waiting for me. Thankfully, he was the only one there.

"You're late."

"My time is not my own, Marlowe. What did the manager say?"

"He thanked me for discovering the items. He didn't like what I said next."

"What did you tell him?"

"That we should leave the items right where they were and see who comes to retrieve them."

"But that could take weeks!"

"I don't think so. That cue is not the most secure of places. Somebody is bound to notice it rattles. He'll want to retrieve the stolen goods sooner rather than later. My guess? He'll make an appearance tonight or tomorrow night at the latest."

"How do you plan to catch him in the act?" It had to be a man as women were not allowed in the club, not even in the kitchen.

"There's a locked cupboard in the billiards room where the more valuable spirits are stored. I'll hide there. None of the members know about it."

"But surely some of the staff do."

"Only three. The club manager, his assistant, and the sommelier. There's only one key to the cupboard which is kept in the manager's office."

"How big is the space?"

"Comfortable enough to accommodate me."

"And you plan to hide there for two days?"

"No. Only nights. It was raining last night, if you'll recall." He quirked a crooked grin.

Which I returned with my one of my own. "Yes, I know." How could I ever forget the image of him soaking wet?

"Unfortunately, the billiards room suffered water damage, so the manager is locking it while they make repairs."

"Umm." Not one of the servers had mentioned such a thing. "There is no damage, is there?"

"Correct. But it has to appear as if there is. The manager will put up a sign to that effect at the entrance to the club and the gents' room. He will also announce that the billiards room will be left open at the end of the day to air it out."

"Laying a trap. Very clever."

He rocked back on his heels. "I thought so."

"Your suggestion?"

"Just so. Would you like to join me tonight?"

"You said there was room for only one person."

"Comfortably. But two can fit, especially if one is as dainty as you."

"I'm of average height and weight for a lady, Marlowe."

"Like I said, dainty. What do you say?"

The offer was awfully tempting. I would love to catch the thief in the act of retrieving the stolen goods. But it would not be an easy thing to arrange. "I'm tempted. But how am I to do this? I'm supposed to leave the premises at eleven."

"Don't worry. I'll arrange it with the manager."

The clock in the library struck the hour. My break was done. "I have to go."

"I'll see you at midnight."

Unless something happened to prevent such a thing.

CHAPTER 8

A DISCUSSION WITH THE MANAGER

That night when my shift ended at eleven, I was called into the club manager's office.

"You think he's unto you?" Mister Clark asked.

"I hope not."

"Whatever you do, don't mention my name," he said, a worried expression on his face.

Totally appropriate. If the manager had discovered I was a female, Mister Clark would most certainly be implicated. After all, I'd been hired on his recommendation. Still, I could offer what reassurance I could. "Don't worry, I won't."

On shaking knees, I walked up the stairs and down the corridor to my destination. I had no doubt Marlowe had discussed his plan with Mister Stafford. The manager could have approved it, or he could have divined I was a female and asked me to his office to dismiss me. Well, there was only one way to find out. Firming my shoulders, I knocked on the door.

THE CASE OF THE STRAY STICKPIN

"Come in," a firm voice commanded.

The club manager, a gentleman in his early fifties, stood behind his desk immaculately attired in an understated but elegant dark suit. The only relief from the unrelenting black was the blinding white of his shirt.

"Good evening, Sir. You asked to see me?"

"Yes, I did." For the longest time, he studied me, carefully, thoroughly, no expression to his face. I hardly dared breathe so intense was his scrutiny. Once he was done, he arched a brow.

Clearly, he knew who I was, or rather what I was. A female. One who'd invaded the hallowed halls of his all male bastion. I did not know what he would do. Would I be dismissed, or ignominiously hauled away? Disastrous, either way. If my role in this investigation was discovered, not only would my reputation be ruined but so would that of the Ladies of Distinction Detective Agency. I anxiously awaited his next words.

"Lord Marlowe has informed me you will be joining him in the billiards room." I breathed a sigh of relief. He'd decided my gender would be ignored. His reason was not hard to determine. He was preserving the sanctity of the club.

"Yes, Sir." As I didn't know what Marlowe had told the manager, the best approach would be to keep my answers to a minimum.

Meticulous to a fault, he shifted a paper on his desk, straightened the ink blot, before addressing me again. "You will remain here in my office until midnight. Lord Marlowe is due to return by then. Once he does, I will escort you both to the billiards room and open the spirits cupboard. You will remain there until seven tomorrow morning when I'll come to check on you." He cleared his throat. "I trust you will conduct yourself in a manner which will not disgrace the club."

Heaven forbid Marlowe and I do anything untoward. "Of course."

His brow arched once more.

CHAPTER 9

A MIDNIGHT ESCAPADE

Shortly before midnight, a knock sounded on the manager's office door. Since I didn't know who it was, I hid behind the massive desk and held my breath while someone stepped into the room.

"Now, where did he go?" I thought it was the manager's voice but wasn't sure.

"You left him here?" Marlowe!

I popped up. "Here I am."

"What the devil are you doing hiding back there?" Marlowe asked.

"I didn't know who was on the other side of the door."

"But I told you," the manager started to say. "Never mind. Let us make our way to the billiards room."

Marlowe and I followed him silently through the club. When we arrived at the billiards room, he unlocked the door and led the way to a spot along the wall. He fetched a key and inserted it into a small hole in a carved rosette. A door swung open revealing a cupboard filled with bottle after bottle of wines, champagne, and other spirits. One thing was missing.

"There's nowhere to sit," I said.

"There's the floor," Marlowe pointed out.

"We'll have to kneel if we want to see out through the keyhole."

"You won't have to do that," the manager said. "I'll leave the door open an inch or so. That should be enough for you to hear someone enter the room."

"But what if the thief sees the open door?" I inquired.

"He won't. The cupboard is situated away from the billiards tables and the rack of cues. It will be dark. Unless he shines a light in your direction, he won't notice the door's ajar."

Marlowe stepped farther into the room and grabbed two cushions from one of the settees. "These will give us a place to seat."

It wasn't the best arrangement, but it was infinitely better than the hard floor.

"Now, as I mentioned before," the manager said, "I shall return in the morning at seven to hear your report."

"What if the thief comes to fetch his ill-gotten goods?"

"Lord Marlowe will apprehend him. He will then telephone my residence, and I will rush over. Under no circumstance are you to notify the police. Is that clear?"

"Yes, Sir," I said.

Marlowe simply nodded.

"And you are not to engage in untoward behavior."

"Don't worry. Your spirits are safe with us," Marlowe said.

"That's not what I meant," the manager said brushing a hand across his troubled brow. "Now I shall go home. It's beyond time I sought my bed."

"Sweet dreams," I said.

"Fitful, more like. Goodnight." And off he went.

THE CASE OF THE STRAY STICKPIN

"I think he knows I'm a female."

"Why do you think that?"

"Untoward behavior?" I reminded him.

His voice rose. "Does he honestly think I'd engage in intimate relations with a woman on the dusty floor of a cupboard?"

"Apparently so."

"Well, he's wrong. I'm too fastidious for that."

"Good to know." I grinned.

Leaning back against a cabinet, we accommodated ourselves on the cushions. By necessity, we kept our conversations to a minimum so we couldn't be detected. As the space was not heated, I was soon shivering from the chill.

"You're cold, aren't you?" Marlowe asked.

"A tad, yes."

"Well, I can't have that." Next thing I knew he was pulling me, cushion and all, close to him.

The word 'untoward' came to mind, and I sought to protest. But I stifled the urge. He was awfully warm.

After an hour, I grew drowsy. Soon, I had my head on Marlowe's chest. I was almost asleep when the sound of something scurrying across bare floor reached me. "What was that?"

"I'm guessing a rat."

"WHAT!!!"

He clamped his hand across my mouth. "Don't scream."

I did as he said while drawing harsh, desperate breaths. I was beyond petrified of long-tailed rodents.

A few seconds later, he removed his hand. "I think it's gone. Your yelling probably chased it away."

I jumped to my feet.

"What the devil are you doing?"

"I have to visit the lavatory."

"You should have taken care of that before."

"I did. But the rat scared—"

"The piss out of you?" He finished somewhat facetiously.

"Don't be crude, Marlowe. It doesn't suit you," I said in my haughtiest voice.

"I apologize. Don't take long and don't make any noise."

I didn't give him the courtesy of an answer. I simply walked out head held high. As quietly as I could, I handled my bodily needs. And then on stockinged feet, I walked back to the billiards room. I didn't make it. A palm clamped around my mouth. Unlike Marlowe's, this one smelled of spirits.

"Where's that man of yours?" A guttural voice demanded.

He's not my man, I wanted to say. But since trying to speak would be useless, I simply shrugged.

"Cat got your tongue, dearie?" he asked.

I said and did nothing. Something hard was pressed to my back. Something that felt like a gun barrel.

His next words confirmed it. "I'm going to remove my hand. If you scream, I'll kill you. Do you understand?"

I nodded.

Once he removed his palm, I was finally able to breathe. "Why are you doing this, Mister Hodgson?" I asked my back still to him.

"How did you guess?"

I turned around to face him. "You called me, dearie, the same as when I first met you. And you smell of spirits. A sommelier would have that on him."

"Especially if he likes the occasional tipple."

"Why are you doing this?" I asked again.

"For the money, of course."

A sly movement to my right alerted me to the presence of another. Marlowe. Desperate to keep Hodgson's attention on me, I challenged him. "You'll never get away with this."

"On the contrary. I've already made arrangements with a

fence. He's waiting for me right now. With the money I receive, I plan to travel far away from merry old England."

"The United States?"

"Wouldn't you like to know, dearie?"

"Duck!" Marlowe yelled.

I dropped to the floor. Something swished above me. A thunk later, Hodgson dropped next to me, his arm outstretched, the gun loose in his hand. I checked his pulse. He was unconscious but breathing.

Marlowe rushed over and carefully retrieved the weapon.

"What did you hit him with?"

"That." He pointed to a cue near us, now broken in two parts.

I jumped to my feet. "I could have been shot."

"But you weren't. Now help me find something to tie him up with."

"The sashes on the curtains."

"Get 'em. I'll keep watch over him."

With my hands trembling as they were, it took several tries to achieve this. When I brought them to Marlowe, he handed me the revolver and proceeded to truss up Mister Hodgson's feet and hands together.

"That looks rather uncomfortable. Is it really necessary?"

He grabbed my shoulders. "He could've killed you. I hope it hurts like the devil." And then he kissed me.

I stiffened, and then, like the ninny I am, I melted into him and kissed him right back. After a few delicious moments, he ended the embrace. Grinning at me, he said, "I knew you were besotted with me."

"Besotted? Think again, Marlowe. It's the danger of the moment. Now what shall we do?"

"Call the manager like he said."

CHAPTER 10

ALL'S WELL THAT ENDS WELL

The club manager arrived half an hour after we contacted him. He'd been expecting the call. So much so, he'd made his bed on a sofa he'd shifted close to his telephone. The question now became what to do with Mister Hodgson.

The manager decided an interrogation would be conducted in his office. Marlowe untrussed Hodgson so he could walk there. But when we arrived, he pushed him into a chair and tied him to it.

"Highly inappropriate behavior, Mister Hodgson," the manager said. "I expect better of my staff."

"You don't pay us enough."

"The club pays the usual rate."

After that exchange, the manager glared at the sommelier. And then breathing a heavy sigh, he said, "I won't charge you with theft."

"Why not?" I asked.

THE CASE OF THE STRAY STICKPIN

"Because I don't want the club involved in his ugly matter, young lady."

I glanced at Marlowe. "Told you he knew."

"I could cut off his hand," Marlowe suggested with an evil grin. "That's what was done to thieves."

Mister Hodgson looked horrified. "I got little ones to feed."

"Likely story," Marlowe said.

"God's truth." He struggled against the rope to hold up his hand but then thought better of it. Probably because he didn't want Marlowe to act on his proposal.

"If you don't charge him with theft," I asked the manager, "what are you planning to do?"

"Unfortunately, there's no help for it," he replied. "We'll have to let him go."

"Thank you, Sir. My wife and little ones thank ye."

"Don't thank me so fast, Mister Hodgson," the manager said. "You'll never get another job in the City of London. At least in one of the finer establishments. I'll make sure every last one of them knows your dastardly behavior."

"He deserves to go to jail," Marlowe protested.

"I quite agree with you, milord," the manager said. "But I don't want Black's involved."

"How did you do it?" I asked Mister Hodgson. "How did you steal all the things you did?"

He puffed up his chest. "Piece of cake. Lord Marlowe's pin? It was loose. When I showed him the wine list, all I had to do was pluck it off him. He didn't feel a thing."

Marlowe mumbled something obscene beneath his breath.

"And the ring?"

"That particular gentleman has dropped a stone or two. Due to illness, as it turns out. He was the one who suffered a turn and was taken to hospital. I noticed his emerald ring was rather loose on his finger. So, when I helped him to his favorite spot in the dining room, I slipped it off him."

"You're despicable."

He shrugged. "Been called worse."

"And the watch?"

"Now that was pure dumb luck. Found it. A loose clasp."

"What about the cash in Lord Nesmith's pocket?"

"I helped myself to it when I brought him another tot of whiskey."

"And he didn't suspect you?"

"Of course he did. He's not stupid. But I'd already stashed the cash. I didn't have it on me."

After that, there was nothing more to say. The manager was kind enough to allow him to gather his things, after he checked them over, before ejecting him from the premises. Marlowe was not so gracious. He delivered a swift kick to the sommelier's hindquarters, causing him to land on all fours on the pavement.

"Well, that's that, I suppose," the manager said. "Thank you, Lord Marlowe. You too, err, Thomas." He did allow himself a small smile when he said my name. "Your services will no longer be required."

"Of course," I said. "It's been an interesting experience, Sir."

A raised brow was his only answer.

After I fetched my belongings, Marlowe offered to escort me home. "My automobile is parked outside."

"You have your pin?" I asked before we left the club.

He retrieved it from his pocket and flashed it at me. Still as ugly as ever, but precious to him.

As we made our way to his vehicle, I said, "Investigation successfully concluded. I'll send you a final reckoning in the morning."

He hauled me into him and kissed me. "It is morning, my dear Lady Emma."

"And so it is," I said and kissed him right back.

∼

IF YOU ENJOYED THIS BOOK, check out the next Kitty Worthington Cozy Caper, **The Case of the Unsuitable Suitor**, Book 3 in this series.

A princess on the verge of a calamitous marriage. A government alliance on the brink of collapse. Can Kitty Worthington put a stop to the nuptials before disaster ensues?

London 1924. When the royal princess of Zenovia falls madly in love with a rake during London's social season, the British government appeals to **Kitty Worthington** for help in exposing the despicable dastard. Her first inclination is to deny the request. As busy as her detective agency is, it would be madness to take on such a task.

But when her fiancé, **Chief Detective Inspector Robert Crawford Sinclair**, is assigned to an undercover operation to investigate the unsuitable suitor, Kitty accepts the government's mandate. After all, she doesn't wish to go weeks without seeing him. The enquiry will demand she alter her looks, move to a new residence, and act in ways she's never acted before. Can she do the impossible without losing everything she holds dear, including herself?

The Case of the Unsuitable Suitor, Book 3 in the Kitty Worthington Cozy Capers, is another delightful historical cozy frolic from the pen of *USA Today* **Bestselling author Magda Alexander**. This captivating tale is replete with intrigue, humor, and a dash of romance. Set in the glamorous world of 1920s London, it's sure to delight readers of Agatha Christie and Downton Abbey alike.

This book is a work of fiction. All names, characters, locations, and incidents are products of the author's imagination, or have been used fictitiously. Any resemblance to actual persons living or dead, locales, or events is entirely coincidental.

Copyright © 2024 by Amalia Villalba

All rights reserved.

The uploading, scanning, and distribution of this book in any form or by any means—including but not limited to electronic, mechanical, photocopying, recording, or otherwise—without the permission of the copyright holder is illegal and punishable by law. Please purchase only authorized editions of this work, and do not participate in or encourage electronic piracy of copyrighted materials. Your support of the author's rights is appreciated.

ISBN-13: (EBook) 978-1-943321-29-2

ISBN-13: (Paperback) 979-8-877836-01-3

Hearts Afire Publishing

First Edition January 2024

CAST OF CHARACTERS

Lady Emma Carlyle - Our amateur sleuth

The Ladies of Distinction Detective Agency

    Kitty Worthington - Agency Partner
    Betsy Robson - Agency Receptionist
    Owen Clapham - former Scotland Yard detective inspector who assists with investigations

Black's - A Gentleman's Club

    Mister Aloysius Clark - Lady Emma's contact and a server at the club
    Mister Hodgson - Club Sommelier
    Mister Stafford - Club Manager
    Club Assistant Manager

Other Notable Characters

CAST OF CHARACTERS

Lord Marlowe - An Earl who hires Lady Emma to search for his missing tie pin

Lord Meecham - An aristocrat who borrows money from Lord Marlowe

Printed in Great Britain
by Amazon